For Rob
and his dolphin friend
Little Bit,
and for Carin, Gladys, and Carm,
who know that we are all One Family.
K.P.

To Gita,
Hannah, Sam, Willis, Madison,
and Katherine.
M.N.

By Day and By Night

Verse by Karen Pandell

Illustrated by Marty Noble

H J Kramer Inc
Starseed Press
Tiburon, California

By day I see the sun.
The sun is me.

By day I see a tree.
The tree is me.

I see a butterfly.
The butterfly is me.

By day I hear a swan.
The swan is me.

I hear the wind.
The wind is me.

By day I hear a wolf.

The wolf is me.

By day I touch a rock.
The rock is me.

I touch a ladybug.
The ladybug is me.

By day I touch a dolphin.

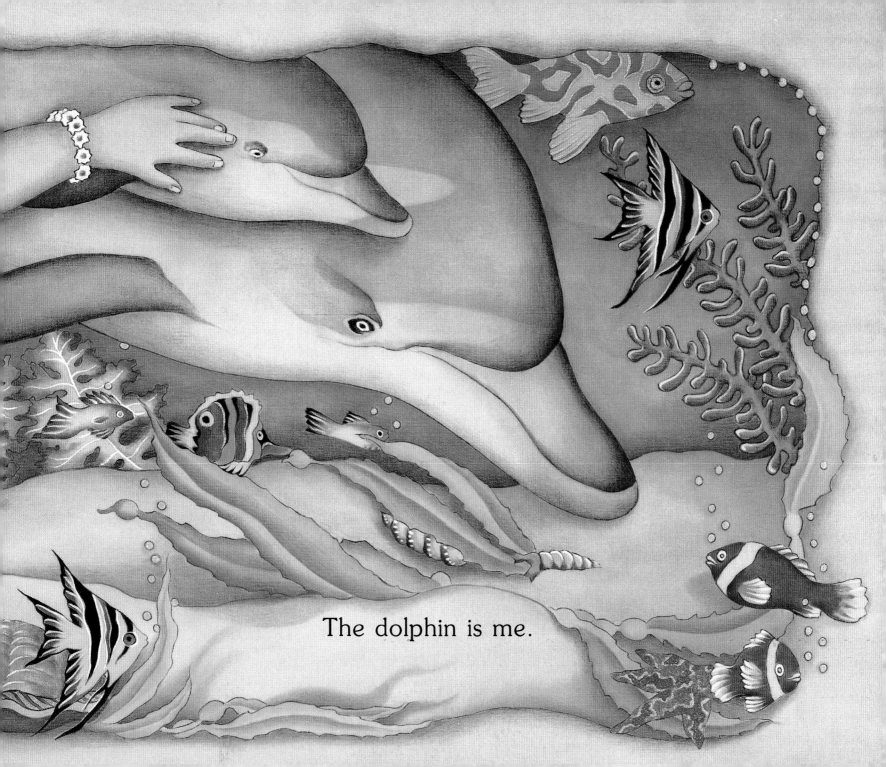

The dolphin is me.

By day I smell a rose.

The rose is me.

By day I smell the sea.

The sea is me.

By day I taste an orange.

The orange is me.

By day I taste the rain.
The rain is me.

By night I watch the moon.

The moon is me.

By night I sip cool water.

The cool water is me.

By night I listen to my favorite story.
My favorite story is me.

By night I feel my soft blanket.
My soft blanket is me.
I sniff my cuddly teddy bear.
My cuddly teddy bear is me.

By day and by night,
I know my world.
My world is one with me.

Text Copyright © 1991 by Karen Pandell
Illustrations Copyright © 1991 by Marty Noble

H J Kramer Inc
P.O. Box 1082
Tiburon, CA 94920

Library of Congress Cataloging-in-Publication Data
Pandell, Karen.
 By day and by night / verse by Karen Pandell ; illustrated by
Marty Noble.
   p.   cm.
 Summary: A child's five senses are activated by many things during
the day and night.
 ISBN 0-915811-26-X
 [1. Senses and sensation – Fiction. 2. Day – Fiction. 3. Night –
Fiction.] I. Noble, Marty, 1948- ill. II. Title.
PZ7.P1888By 1991   90-52635
[E] – dc20   CIP
                                                        AC

Art Director: Linda Kramer
Book Production: Schuettge and Carleton
Typesetting: Classic Typography
10 9 8 7 6 5 4 3 2 1
Printed in Hong Kong